Blink

Ian Rowlands is a playwright and director whose work has been at the forefront of Welsh drama in English and Welsh since the emergence of his first plays in the early 1990's. He trained at the Welsh College of Music and Drama before becoming a founding member of Theatr Y Byd where he wrote and directed a series of innovative plays, including *Marriage of Convenience* which won an Angel award at the Edinburgh Festival and the best play award at the Dublin Theatre Festival. He has also written successfully for television and radio, notably winning a Royal Society of Television Award for drama *A Light in the Valley*.

Blink

Ian Rowlands

Parthian
The Old Surgery
Napier Street
Cardigan
SA43 1ED

www.parthianbooks.co.uk

First published in 2008
© Ian Rowlands 2008
All Rights Reserved

ISBN 978-1-905762-85-9

Cover design by Lucy Llewellyn
Inner design & typsetting by books@lloydrobson.com
Additional by Lucy Llewellyn
Printed and bound by Lightning Source

Published with the financial support of the Welsh
Books Council

British Library Cataloguing in Publication Data – A
cataloguing record for this book is available from the
British Library

First performed at Chapter Arts Centre, Cardiff
30 October 2007

Cast:

Si	–	Sion Pritchard
Mam	–	Lisa Palfrey
Kay	–	Rhian Blythe

Creative Team:

Director	–	Stephen Fisher
Producer	–	Emma Goad
Production Manager	–	Sarah Cole
Designer	–	Rhys Jarman
Lighting Designer	–	Trevor Turton
Sound Designer	–	Gareth Potter
Company Stage Manager	–	Sharlene Harvard Young
Technical Stage Manager	–	Stephen Hawkins

Co-produced by F.A.B. & Torch theatre companies

Originally read as part of the *On the Edge* season
Chapter Arts Centre, Cardiff, 2007

Cast:

Si	–	Nathan Sussex
Mam	–	Sharom Morgan
Kay	–	Maria Pride

Creative Team:

Director – Michael Kelligan

Filmed for BBC 2W, 2006

Cast:

Si	–	Richard Harrington
Mam	–	Sharon Morgan
Kay	–	Maria Pride

Creative Team:

Ian Rowlands, Dean Arnott, Maggie Rusell

Written with the assistance of a bursary
from Arts Council Wales.

To the friends I know, and to all the friends I will never know, who have endured and continue to endure but survive.

In memory of Peter Clarke
(Children's Commissioner for Wales), who believed

ONE

A woman, MAM sits beside an hospital bed. Her son, SI, cleans a pair of shoes. His girlfriend, KAY, assembles a wreath. It reads, 'Dad we ♡ U'. In the bed lies a fourth character, DAD. He remains silent throughout – a strain for such an outspoken man! He is attached to a life support machine. For a while they sit in silence. Time; no time like the present, as my Mam used to say!

SI: I was sitting in the Balham Hotel, gateway to nowhere, just sitting there with Syke that Saturday afternoon; Kempton on TV, the bar was glued to it. Go on Prodigal Son... go on you bastard! Bugger it! Balham Hotel, losers' hell, but we got lucky that day...

SI and KAY dovetail on 'that day'.

KAY: ... that day I called for him on my own. Which was odd, because I only ever used to call for him with Debbie. She was eight, Si was six, I was five; the tag-along kid of the Rudey Club, that was me. The three of us'd sit behind bushes waiting to jump up naked and scare pensioners half to death. If we'd have been older, I reckon we would all've been ECT'd!

SI: What's your name? I asked, first time I met him. Syke, he said. How do you spell that? S-Y-K-E, he said, I've dropped the O. Oh, I said, Psycho! Mad fuck, mad family.

KAY: It was summer. His front door had this deck-chair thing going on to stop it fading in the sun; big thing in the Valleys before double-glazing.

SI: One day...

SI and KAY dovetail:

SI: His *brother* answered the door...

KAY: His *mother* answered the door...

SI: To a couple of dealers who shot half his face away for the sake of a principle. Syke got out of the valley fast, his principles were too pretty to lose. Ugly git!

KAY: Oh, hello Kay, she said. That's a lovely dress you're wearing; cool like a daffodil. Thank you, Mrs Voel.

SI: Anyway, that morning, he'd just hitched the M4 into Knightsbridge. A lorry dropped him off outside Harrods. I've got this lucky feeling about London, he said, bumming a floor for the night. As if one night was all he would stay! But he was right, because we were sitting in the Balham Hotel when this woman walked across the bar, all short skirts and legs like plucked chickens, laughing to herself 'cause shit happens, and why not. Anyway, she smiled at us, we smiled back. Then she lifted up her skirt and flapped it. Lick a bit of that? she said. Cut price, two up! My father'd turn in his grave. If only he'd have the decency to lie in it.

KAY: How's your mum's legs? She asked. They play hell, she says, I said. Shame, and she was such a lovely dancer down The Rink as well! Look who's here to see you, Si. And Si looked at me as if I was something the cat'd just dragged in. I'll leave you two to play, she said. But as soon as her back was turned, Rudey Club, he whispered. Rudey Club...

SI: Lick a bit of that.

MAM: (*Talking to DAD*) I came on the bus today, love... hell of a journey... it always takes longer in the rain. And I was thinking. Remember, Bri? Remember our first date? Remember that? Have you ever ridden before? you said. No, I said, and we shot off on your bike; up the forest, dodging ruts. My heart was in my mouth. In my mouth, it was. Just hold on tight! you screamed. Thirty years hanging on by the skin of my teeth... thirty years... gone like that... doesn't bear thinking about, does it...

KAY: And he led me up the garden path to his dad's garage – all oily and dusty. And he watched as I took down my knickers and stood there naked, dust swirling around me. Can I smell it? he asked. And he got on his knees and put his nose between my legs. It smells of pee, he said. Can I touch it? Can I?

MAM: Remember, Bri? We rode to the top of the tip, and you pulled a gun out of that long bag you made me carry on my back, and you shot a crow. And it exploded in mid-air. Whap! (*She claps her hands to illustrate.*) Gone, like bubbles in the bath. Poor little bugger. What did you do that for, Bri? Don't be such a woman, you said. What else am I supposed to be? Eh? That gun went towards the wedding ring, didn't it? But you never got rid of your cruel streak. Did you? It's in your nature to kill, isn't it, Bri?

SI: Anyway, on the way back to Boundaries Road, I was telling Syke about the time the Balham Tube Strangler was arrested in our back garden, when my mobile rang, and it was my brother. Which was odd because he never used to ring up to say Jack-shit. And his voice was all quiet like, as if he was the big bro and I was the little kid. I think you'd better come home, he said, it's Dad. Something's happened. And, to be honest, I didn't give a toss. Five years away, I didn't want to eat the fatted calf just yet. For Mam, he said. The bastard!

MAM: We had a lovely wedding down the Con though, didn't we? Fair do's. And all our friends were there, and all the old women you'd see at every wedding and funeral. God knows who they were! Beats bingo, I suppose. And then the reception up the Res. And they did us proud, didn't they? Everybody said it was a lovely spread. And we danced... off my feet I was; perfect. Apart from when your ex whispered in my ear, I hope all your kids die of cancer. I was pregnant with Simon at the time, wasn't I? And I turned round, and if it wasn't for the fact that it was my big day, I swear to God, I would've slapped her one. Can't you take a joke, love? she said, tottering off. I never forgave her; never. Even when I saw her a few years after that, in a wheelchair, crippled with arthritis. It's just going from bad to worse, she said, no cure. Well, you reap what you sow, love, I thought, you reap what you bloody well sow....

Simon was perfect, thank God, but if he hadn't have been, I swear now, Bri, I would've gone round her house and crippled her myself. Cow! But, thank God, Si was a lovely baby, wasn't he? Not like his brother – little bugger; up all hours, up to all sorts. Simon was gorgeous. I loved him from the moment I clapped eyes on him. Saw him before you did, you used to say, saw the top of his head in your hole. It was like bloody Vietnam down there! Yes. Thank you, Brian!

KAY: The tip of his finger barely touching me. Like touching shit with a stick...

MAM: And, you know, after all the pain, that's all I could think of, lying in that hospital bed, was one day, my little baby was going to die. And Si looked so gorgeous lying in my arms; like a little Jesus, he was. And I should've been over the moon, but that's all I could think of was, one day, he's just going to die. And I thought, why? All the pain'd mean nothing in the end... nothing... all the pain. I'm not saying you raped me, Bri, I'm not saying that... I wouldn't say that... it's just you took me too soon after the birth, Bri, and it felt like... it felt...

KAY: Warm, like a dog, he said... poking me. I was about eight when Si moved to the other side of the Valley. We'd bump into each other in Hannah Street when we'd be out shopping with our mams. Si should come over and play with Kay, my mum'd say. You've missed him, haven't you love? Dead embarrassed!

Then, one day, he cycled over on his brand new big boy's bike, too big for his feet to touch the floor. He thought he was chocolate on it. And we were playing at the bottom of the street, with clothes on! And I remember he was wearing a black leather bomber jacket his father had just bought him down Ponty market. And he was so proud of it, and extra careful in case it got scratched. Then, down the hill, past Lewis' bakery, we saw the Evans'; the smelly family; ten bad smells in one house, they stank Mary Street out. They saw us and we panicked as they ran towards us. Well, I got away, but Si struggled uphill on his big boy's bike. His foot slipped off the pedal and he scraped his shin. And he was crying when they caught up with him, slapping him on the back of his brand new Ponty bomber jacket. They circled him like Indians, but he had no fight in him, so they got bored and went off to stink another street out. He couldn't look at me after that, he just took off; said nothing. He threw his leather jacket into the river on his way home. The Evans' had marked it with their filth, he said... years later. I blame his mother, she was a stickler for germs. You know, she once disinfected a Bible he'd bought at a chapel jumble! She cotton balled him, would've freeze dried him like an herb, if she could've! Shame, 'cause he never came over again...

SI: And I just knew... I had this gut feeling. I could hear the crows laughing; bastard Valley's crows in London. And as I put the phone off, this girl passed me. And she looked at me, and she was the spit of Kay; the dead spit; same hair, same eyes, same everything...

KAY: What hurt me most was when he used to walk past me in school as if I was the Invisible Woman. Though, to be honest, I barely existed for myself. Nobody expected much of me, so I expected even less of myself. I drifted through school like a ghost. Two school photos taken during my time at the Comp. I'm not in either of them. It's as if I was never there. Then, in the fourth form, I got a Saturday job here in the florist, and I loved it straight off. Natural flair, Sheila said. And I was chuffed to bits, because at last I could do something. And it wasn't a case of 'Kay must try harder', I could do it with my eyes tight shut, as if I'd been born for it. I loved the smell of lilies... all pollen stains on my school dress... and roses.... Then one Saturday, I was arranging a four-foot long 'Dad, we ♡ U' in yellow carnations, when he walked into the shop...

Together:

SI: Kay...

KAY: Kay... (*she remembers*) he said, I want a red rose. Would you like some fern? Ribbons? What about a card? Whatever, he said. And I wrapped a single rose – not the best in the shop because I hated the thought of him buying a red rose for anyone else. Would you like to write a message on the

8

card before I staple it? Aye, all right, he said, and he wrote, 'Will you go out with me?' on the card then handed it back. That'll be one pound fifty, I said, jealous as hell. He handed me the money, I gave him the rose. No, keep it, he said, it's for you. And that's all I could think of was why hadn't I wrapped the best rose in the shop? Why hadn't I wrapped the best rose in the bloody shop!

SI: I thought for a bit I'd have to ask Fat Janet who'd do it with anyone...

KAY: We were first loves...

SI: First time we did it, we were babysitting Steve, Kay's little brother; little bastard. He wouldn't go to sleep, would he. Shut up or I'll fart in your face, I said. And he hated it when I did that. He'd pull this jib like a kid eating a lemon! Twat! Then when we were sure he was fast asleep...

KAY: I could feel him through his trousers, hard against my breast...

SI: Felt like I was going to burst...

KAY: He undid his zip and pressed my hand against him. He was pushing and I didn't know what was happening...

SI: Bursting...

KAY: And then he came...

SI: She thought I was bleeding...

KAY: I thought I'd hurt him...

SI: She cried...

KAY: So sticky...

SI: Sticky, she said...

KAY: Frightened me...

SI: Frightened her. We did it proper later, dunkie and all, and we did it quick before her mam and dad came back from the pub. Then it was my turn to look. But there was nothing; no blood, nothing. Horse riding, she said...

KAY: Scared me...

SI: And I know it's stupid, but I felt cheated, you know. I wanted blood. But, shit, it could've been worse, I guess. It could've been Fat Janet up the back lane for a sausage and a bag of chips. I love you, we said, falling into our trousers... I love you, Kay...

KAY: And the top of his thing was scarlet and swollen, like a rose; like a blood-red rose, it was....

TWO

SI: I reckon the big moments, the important things that shape our lives, could probably be squashed into a day. No; less than a day – a few hours. No, less than that even; just a few minutes. A few poxy minutes out of a whole life. All those bits of memory, like photograph's on the mantle-piece. Never quite sure if they ever happened, always shagged from their effect.

KAY: He said he loved me?

MAM: After all we'd sacrificed for him. And nothing we said would change his mind, would it, Bri? Nothing! Such a waste it was, because he had everything going for him, everything. We expected so much from him, so much.... Always expect the worse, I suppose; Valley's expectations, that way you don't get disappointed, do you. I'm going to London, he said. What the hell for, love? For God's sake, Brian, say something! Leave now kid, and don't you ever set foot in this house again! You were always all heart, Bri. Trouble is, wherever your heart was, you always put your foot in it.

KAY: You're hurting me...

SI: She said, why are you leaving, Si? (*To KAY*) I don't want to leave, Kay.

KAY: You'll ruin everything.

SI: I know.

KAY: Three years down the drain.

SI: I know.

KAY: Stay then.

SI: I can't.

KAY: Why?

SI: Can't explain.

KAY: Try.

SI: It's nothing.

KAY: Stop saying nothing. Just tell me.

SI: I can't, I'm sorry.

KAY: You're not sorry. And you don't care. I hate you!

SI: Yeah, well...

KAY: You're just a little shit, and I never want to see you again!

MAM: And I went to see that Arfon Jones after Si left. Thought he might've said something to his teacher before leaving, but... nothing. I wish I could help you more, he said. And he was so genuine; butter wouldn't melt; so genuine.

KAY: Is it something I've done?

SI: Nothing.

MAM: I really thought he cared.

KAY: Is it someone else then?

SI: What!

MAM: I trusted him.

KAY: Are you sure?

SI: Don't be so stupid.

MAM: Goes to show, doesn't it.

KAY: Why are you so uptight then?

SI: You're doing my head in, just leave it there...

KAY: We're first loves, Si.

SI: I know.

KAY: Don't that mean anything?

SI: It does, but...

KAY: But what?

SI: But nothing. It means everything, it's just...

KAY: Just what?

SI: Just nothing. Look, leave it, Kay. Please.

MAM: Wolf in bloody sheep's clothing!

Pause.

KAY: Well, if you're going to be such a bastard, I've got news for you as well.

SI: Have you?

KAY: Want to know what it is?

SI: If you want to tell me, tell me.

KAY: It's probably best I don't though.

SI: Don't then.

KAY: I don't want to hurt you.

SI: It's not a game, Kay.

KAY: Who's playing? Do you want to know what it is, or not?

SI: If you want.

KAY: Oh, I want.

SI: Go on then.

KAY: But, I'd better not.

SI: Just tell me, Kay.

KAY: All right, don't say I didn't warn you. Truth is, Si, you've never made me come when you're inside me... not once.

Pause.

SI: Sorry? (*He is thrown.*)

KAY: I've always pretended; never wanted to hurt you.

SI: Saving the hurt up, were you?

KAY: You started it.

SI: Great. Look, to be honest, I don't care.

KAY: I think you do.

SI: Yesterday, but not today.

KAY: What's different today?

SI: It's Shitsday.

KAY: You said it! I thought coming at the same time was a sign of true love.

SI: Looks like a sign I should go then.

MAM: He was such a charming man, that Arfon Jones was; a real gentleman! Thank you for all the help and advice you've given my Simon, it's meant a lot to him, I said as I left. I did, I thanked him, Bri... I actually thanked him, that's what I did. I wish I could suck those words back into my mouth, suck them back in like an 'oover. Wish I'd never said them... I wish... oh God... want a grape, love?

THREE

SI: Balham. Gateway to the South. And me a boy from Porth, gateway to nowhere. Sort of synchronicity. Mine for the taking....

I've only ever seen Wales from a train window, Connor said, opening the door to the room-for-rent. If there's a smell, sorry, my cat's just shat on the bed. Great! Downstairs, I was grilled. Fair's fair, I could've been anyone. Taffy was a Welshman, Taffy was a thief, Taffy took a room in Balham and boiled a cat to death. Forty pounds a week and fifty bond. I was landed; one suitcase and a bit of baggage; everybody brings baggage to London, it's the done thing. When can you move in? Now?

That first night I sat in the bare room; no chairs, one mattress and a small cupboard too big for the big nothing I'd brought with me; Valley boy in the big city! I did all sorts. Checked videos, stacked shelves, sold ice cream – Loseley's, only the best! And one day Connor said they were looking for ushers at Riverside Studios. And I remember when this big actor came to tea; best china and cakes. I ate the crumbs off his plate and from the ashtray I nicked one of his butts – Turkish blend, no filter – and I kept it flat in my wallet for months until I gave it to Carol on our first date. She was an actress, thought I'd impress...

KAY: Si thought he was so big. But I'd bounced back even before he'd had a chance to throw me down.

SI: It's for the best, Kay.

KAY: I know, Si. So where are you phoning me from then?

SI: Baker Street.

KAY: That's nice for you.

SI: Is someone with you?

KAY: Sherlock Holmes. End of conversation.

SI: Kay? Kay? Shit.

MAM: (*Takes out half a bag of Maltesers*) Don't look at me with those eyes...

SI: Carol lived above a kebab shop in Tooting Bec. The room stank of donner and Peter Stuyvesant – red. She blew smoke rings and I pierced them with my fag. Why wouldn't you let me kiss you where it counts? She said. It's late, I said, stubbing the butt out...

KAY: We were so happy...

SI: Stubbing her out...

KAY: Craig and me – beauty and the beast. He danced around my handbag, protecting me from all the dogs who hung around smelling meat. We were going serious as well, everybody said we were made for each other. Made for everyone, me! After a few months we made more than we bargained for, but I didn't want to stop dancing, so I kept smoking, hoping for a miscarriage. Then when I lost hope of that, I smoked for a small baby so it'd slip out; I'd get my figure back quick. Ryan was born all scrawny and yellow. Sicky little baby he was. I can never forgive myself for that and I pray every night to God to make my little boy grow up tall and strong in spite of his bad mother! We called him Ryan, after Ryan Giggs. Craig was a massive fan. And we got married, because it was expected of us. And for our wedding we were given eleven knitted bonnets, a cot and a pram...

MAM: What about that time we had lunch in the Brit. Your treat on our anniversary. Remember? Treat by God! Half way through my scampi and chips, she walked in. If she did! And you just couldn't pass up the opportunity, could you? For God's sake, Brian, you were with your wife and son! I saw you, all James Bond at the bar, made me sick. So I stormed out dragging Simon with me. What's wrong, love? you said, coming after me. And that cow hobbled out on

17

twin towers after us. And in the car park, I couldn't help myself, everything came to a head; everything! I'm ashamed when I think of it, what you made me do... be! Not that it was the first time, nor the last, but no more... no more. And she just stood there, shameless cow, with her arm around Simon, comforting him. It'll be all right, love! Poor Simon was bawling his eyes out and a crowd had gathered to gawk – Valley's pass time bloody gawking! And you were shouting pull yourself together, woman. But it was the sight of her patting Simon's head like a dog that really got me, so I went for the bitch – ten years younger, firmer breasts, no grapefruit legs. Slag! And you were trying to part us when you'd brought us so close, so bloody close... (*she folds the empty Maltesers packet*) all gone... empty...

SI: Carol drifted into Lizzie. Lizzie – Chrissy, Chrissy – Debbie, Debbie – Lucy; a new one every year, like a Man U strip. But things always broke up, broke down. And then I'd think of Kay again and I'd miss...

MAM: I missed him so much...

SI: Missed her. I avoided Victoria like the plague, in case I got the urge to jump on a bus, especially at Christmas when...

Together:

SI: ...most people go home to see the family...

MAM: ...most people go home to see the family...

Uncouple.

MAM: ...at Christmas time.

18

SI: Not me.

MAM: It was then I missed Si the most. But I didn't show you. Didn't dare show you. He'd send a card and a present but always forget to send himself.

SI: New Christmas, new family.

MAM: And all day long I'd wonder where was he? What he was doing? Who he was with? Did he miss us? Did he have turkey?

SI: And they'd all think of me as a future son-in-law. But I knew that that Christmas would be my one and only around their Christmas tree, drinking their Tesco's best sherry, burning fag stains in their chairs.

MAM: Those were the quiet Christmases where nothing was said. Brian's law; silent days, silent nights.

Pause.

KAY: It was after the Boxing Day derby, somewhere north of the city, that he lost control. The police never worked out why the car spun across the central reservation. It was a write-off. The two in the back pulled through, but Craig and his friend were killed outright. That was one Christmas present I could've done without, I can tell you!

MAM: He'd send a card, but always forget to send himself!

KAY: The funeral was in Ponty crem, just before the New Year. The biggest one in years, they said. Like one of those old chapel funerals – packed inside, and hundreds outside in Top Man's best and borrowed black ties. Lovely wreath, his best friend said. You've done him proud; a proud widow before I was twenty! Christ! For ages I kept everything as he'd left it; kept his clothes in the wardrobe, sent Christmas cards in both our names. Presents, 'To Ryan from Mam and Dad' as if Craig would come home one day, just walk in through the door...

MAM: I'd watch the New Year come in on TV, hoping to spot him in Trafalgar Square...

KAY: I knew this girl once who watched her boyfriend die of a brain tumour. Twenty-four, he was. Twenty-four! Poor sod. His head swelled up like a balloon. In the end she wasn't allowed in, he didn't want her to see him like that. At least my Craig died tidy.

SI: And in all the time I was in London, I never found the right shoes to wear. The night before my brother rang we were on the King's Road, Chelsea. I was wearing Shoepervalue, Lucy was wearing Russel and Bromley! We'd been together for a year and a half by then – bit of a record. Lucy's dad was a Harley Street doctor; lived in Osterly – big house, swimming pool. I was a Valley's boy who barely kept his head above water. By then I kept a coffee stand in Balham tube and I was sort of doing all right, not in her league though, and her dad made that crystal.

Anyway, that night, the idea was we'd have a quiet drink then back to Balham. But things didn't work out as we'd planned. We were talking politics – always a mistake. I got on my high horse about the usual. It was her accent, location-location twang, and her bloody shoes, I couldn't help myself. Lucy just sat there, saying nothing. By then, she'd learnt not to argue back when I was on a roll. But her saying nothing just made things worse. So I got up to get another drink. You don't need another pint, Simon, she said. Oh, I do, Lucretia, I said. And I was standing at the bar when I thought sod it, and changed my order. Give me a jug of Pimms and two glasses, I said. And I dumped the jug on the table. Here, drink this, I said, It's more your style, you and your fucking family who diss me because I'm a sheep-shagging shit. I don't know why the hell you stay with me. Is it because you pity me? Is that it? Your bit of rough before the taffeta and silk! Just drink your Pimms and get out of my life. Cheers and fuck off....

What a twat! I don't know what the hell came over me because I really liked her, at least I wanted to be like her; easy and English with shoes to fit any occasion. Comfortable walking down any street.

Call me when you get better, she said, leaving me, walking away with Russel and bastard Bromley. But I never called her. She never called me. You can always tell a man by his shoes, my mam used to say. Bastard Shoepervalue! Bastard!

SI places the pair of shoes he has polished to a mirror shine upon his feet. MAM holds a photograph.

MAM: Bri. Don't know why I carry this old photograph around with me, but I think you're actually happy here, Bri. Ken took this one, didn't he? Just after you'd parked your new van outside our house. Your brand new van, full of brand new tools, and on all the handles you had your name printed. Brian Voel and Son. Master Plumber! You were so proud. Well, you know what my mam used to say, eh!

The night they stole your precious van, they might as well have killed you... killed us both. It would've been a mercy killing! Because every morning after that, you'd go down the police station to see if there was any news about your precious van, but there never was, was there? They don't give a shit about us little people, you'd say. Calm

21

down, now Bri, think of your blood presure. Blood pressure my arse! And you'd go on and on and on like a stuck record. It was a Wednesday, wasn't it. It threatened rain so I pulled the clothes in. Goodbye, you said on your way out. Goodbye; not back now, back in a tic, back in a mo, but goodbye. Funny word, I thought, goodbye. But I sort of liked the sound of it...

KAY: I thought Si's dad had fallen. He was lying on the zebra crossing, top of Porth Hill, clutching his chest like a cowboy in the films. So I went over and said who he was. Because Mr Voel, who always had an answer for everything, couldn't even answer with his name. What's wrong with that man, Mammy? He's just tired love, I said. Is he asleep, Mam? Is he asleep like Daddy? Not yet, love, not yet.

SI: For Mam, he said. The bastard! So I put on my Shoepervalue's best, caught the bus out of Victoria and Syke got his bed for the night. And no wanking, right!

FOUR

SI sees MAM and approaches cautiously.

SI: Mam?

MAM: God, you gave me a shock, love.

SI: Sorry.

MAM: Did your brother meet you at the bus stop all right?

SI: No, I got the train up.

MAM: You'd better ring him then, you know what he's like.

SI: Yeah, I will.

They look at each other.

MAM: Look at you. Come here, love... come here.

They embrace.

MAM: You've lost weight. Hasn't she been feeding you?

SI: Who?

MAM: That girl of yours. What's her name?

SI: She's not my mother.

MAM: Glad to hear it. (*Smiles as she looks at him.*) But you look pasty.

SI: I'm all right.

MAM: Are you ill?

SI: Just tired. Tired.

MAM: Your bed's made up; bedroom's just as you left it. I thought we'd lost you, love; thought I'd never see you again...

SI: Well, here I am.

MAM: Your hair still smells like you; sweaty, like when you were a baby.

SI: Great.

MAM: (*An audible half cry*) Oh Si...

SI: You OK, mam?

MAM: Oh, love... (*realises her tears are dripping on his shirt*) all over your shirt. I'll wash it when we get home...

SI: It's OK.

MAM: I'm sorry...

She gathers herself and they pull part.

SI: How is he?

MAM: He'll be pleased you came. You know what he's like. He won't show it, but he will be.

SI: Sure.

MAM: You should've come sooner though love; rang more often.

SI: I've been busy.

MAM: Too busy for your mam...

SI: Mam, I've only just got here...

MAM: I know. Just saying, love...

SI: Yeah.

MAM: Six years is a long time though...

SI: I know.

MAM: A lot of explaining...

SI: Not now.

MAM: Worried myself sick...

SI: Sure.

MAM: You've no idea...

SI: I'm sorry.

MAM: I thought so many things...

SI: I'm back now though.

MAM: You'll be the death of me you will; you will, the death of me . (*She smiles.*)

SI: So what did the doctor say then?

MAM: Fifty-five's not old these days, he said. Ten years of work left in him, more, if he makes a full recovery.

SI: That's OK then.

MAM: Could be worse. They'll have to keep him in for a while though... for observation. He'll be better off here for the time being.

SI: Right

MAM: To be honest, I couldn't cope with him on my own, Si.

SI: Sure.

MAM: I couldn't lift him...

SI: No.

MAM: Too heavy...

SI: Yeah.

MAM: Go and see him now. His eyes lit up when I said you might be coming. I'll wait for you here.

SI: OK.

MAM: And smile.

SI: I won't be long.

MAM: Take as long as you like.

SI walks, then turns.

SI: It's good to be home, Mam.

MAM: Is it, love? Is it?

SI sits in front of the monitor.

SI: How do you pick up a conversation after six years when

the chat was never that great? What the hell do you say to the near dead? When I die, I want to die alone so that no one can look after me out of guilt. I want to die a hermit in a big big city. Forgotten. Not like him. Not like my dad, laid out like a still life, dead fucking still, and life seeping out of him; acid out of a battery.

As I sat there, I kept thinking things. A letter I got from Connor after he'd moved back to Dublin. I'd written to him after he left Balham, wishing him all the best, said I might fly over, because he turned out to be a great bloke, could've killed his cat though. Nearly did one night, with a lump of blow, but that's another story. Anyway, months passed, but no reply from Connor, and I thought fair's fair. Then about a year later I got a letter back from him: sorry I haven't written but I've been in a coma for six months. Simple as that; life lost in the blink of an eye. (*He clicks his fingers.*) Like that.

And a radio interview I heard on the bus on the way home. This SAS bloke. I'm from the sort of family, he said, that if I'd said to my father I love you, he probably would've beaten me with a fist; a hard love – for your own good. Peas sucked to death because you can't leave the table until you swallow them or Dad'll love you with a slap.

But my dad was fifty-five and slapped out. How would he show his love now? A clip round the ear never hurt no one. Wrong, it kills and the pain never dies, but love dies and I'd always wanted him dead. And in his hospital bed, he lay there accusing with silence.

Where in God's name have you been? Your mother's been worried sick. You selfish bastard! He would've said, if he could've slapped my face raw. But silence was thick as Tate and fucking Lyle! Hope you get better soon, Dad, I said as I left. His eye shone defiant and I got out of there quick.

MAM: Was he pleased to see you?

27

SI: Don't know.

MAM: Probably was. You can tell by his eyes. He's missed you, you know. You've always been his favourite.

SI: Ma-am...

MAM: That's not to say that he doesn't think the world of Kevin as well, but you're the first.

SI: Means nothing.

MAM: Means the world to him. He loves you, Si. You know that.

SI: Funny way of showing it.

MAM: He's always been a funny bugger, you know what he's like. It's his way. Do you want more bread and butter with that, love?

SI: No thanks.

MAM: It'll only go to waste.

MAM puts the bread on his plate. SI is about to protest, but...

SI: Thanks.

MAM: By the way, Kay says hello.

SI: Kay?

MAM: Did you see the lovely flowers by your dad's bed?

SI: Yeah.

MAM: She sent them.

SI: Did she?

MAM: She was there.

SI: Where?

MAM: On the bridge, when he collapsed; she saw it all, happened to be passing with Ryan.

SI: Ryan?

MAM: Her kid. Remember? I told you.

SI: Did you?

MAM: In a letter, I know I did.

SI: Did you?

MAM: You never read them, did you?

SI: How old's the kid?

MAM: Thought so.

SI: How old?

MAM: Four, maybe five. Yeah, must be five by now. Bringing a little one up on her own; can't be easy. Anyway, she says hello. Says you should pop into the shop if you get a chance.

SI: I won't be home that long.

MAM: You've only just got here.

SI: It's work. I'll lose it if I stay.

MAM: Tell me again what you do now?

SI: A barista.

MAM: A barrister?

SI: I wish.

MAM: You what?

SI: A barista.

MAM: What's that?

SI: A coffee maker.

MAM: You work in a cafe?

SI: I've got my own stand, down the tube.

MAM: I said you looked pasty, didn't I? No sun. (*Pause*) It's a job of sorts, I suppose.

SI: Keeps me busy.

MAM: But you could've made something of your life, Si.

SI: I have.

MAM: I mean 'something'.

SI: I do all right.

MAM: Look at your shoes.

SI: What about them?

MAM: I worry about you.

SI: You don't have to.

MAM: I'm your mother. I've got no choice. (*Pause.*) Why did you leave like that, Si?

SI: Not now, Mam....

MAM: Why did you leave, love?

SI: Leave it, please Mam.

MAM: Why couldn't you talk about it?

SI: There was nothing to talk about.

MAM: Six years is a long time for nothing, love.

SI: I said not now.

MAM: If your dad was here now...

SI: If he was here, I'd be gone.

MAM: Don't say that.

SI: It's true, Mam. I'm sorry, but it is.

MAM: I'm sorry too, love.... Sorry. (*A breath.*) Do you want ice cream for afters?

SI: Um...

MAM: It's Mr Creamy, your favourite.

SI: No thanks.

MAM: Have a scoop. Go on. You used to live off the stuff.

SI: One scoop then.

MAM: Mr Creamy always asks about you as well.

SI: How is he?

MAM: Hanging on. That's all most people seem to do around here, hanging on.

FIVE

SI: One night, I met an old school friend down the Colliers. I'd gone down for a quiet pint. I was sitting in the corner on my tod, when he came over. He was a couple of years younger than me in school, but I knew him because we both did drama. And he was all, Remember her? Remember him? And I didn't want to remember anyone, but he was Mr Memory and he made the past live again. He told me stuff I didn't want to know; all sorts of shit I didn't want to talk about, but there was no stopping Chuckie. He just spewed it out. And I had no choice but to sit there and get splattered with it.

Told me things... things I believed, but didn't want to believe, though I knew they were true. You wouldn't believe him if he told you. Well you might, but you'd think: fucked-up kid. And you'd want to hear the other side, the grown-up side, thinking the kid lied. But shit happens where you least expect it, even in the tidiest streets.

At least, I suppose, after that, I realised I wasn't alone. I'd always guessed I wasn't, but I wasn't sure who else had suffered until he told me his story, and the stories of boys and girls I knew. One, buggered at eleven! All in the name of drama. If you want to be a great actor, you must experience everything. That was what Arfon Jones used to say. Twelve words that ruined a life; more lives than I'd realised; a real-life fucking tragedy, and I had a scene to add to it, but I didn't want to perform it that night in the Colliers over a pint. So I cut him short, swapped numbers and said I'd ring him. Would I mind if he passed my number onto the police, he asked. They were building up a case on him. Fine, I said, downed my pint and got out of there quick.

MAM: I didn't mind you killing me, Bri. What hurt me most was when you killed Si. Not out of love either, but out of hate; just to teach him a lesson. That's why he did all that drama – to escape from you. And I encouraged him, 'cause I could see his confidence grow until he didn't care what you said to him. And when I saw him grow strong, it made me strong, so I egged him on all the more.... And it was all my fault... all my fault.

SI: Night after night hunched in a corner of the Colliers over a book – 'Kai Lung Unrolls His Mat' – anything to obliterate. Blokes on their way to the bar would say, remember me to your dad? but I'd always forget. And Mr fucking Memory'd ask if the police had rung yet? Twat! Then one night, I saw a face I'd once farted in. Kay's little brother, Steve. Hadn't seen him in years. He caught my eye. Sorry to hear about your dad, he said. Thanks, I said. Tell your sister I'll try and pop round. I didn't mean it, I just said it, he nodded. I nodded.

And the more I sat in the Colliers by night and in the hospital by day I could feel my life slipping. Slowly I was being sucked back into the black like a skinhead's cock up a cow's arse.

KAY: I'd seen him slow down as he'd walk pass, each time slower than the last, staring straight ahead. Then one day he passed slower than ever, almost stopped and I thought, this is stupid! So I rushed to the door but, by the time I stood outside on the pavement, he'd gone. Must've turned down the lane. I couldn't follow him; couldn't leave the shop unlocked....

SI: I stopped in the alley, half expecting. I stood there for ages, waiting... but nothing. Sod it! I thought, this is stupid. Kay knew me better than anyone. We were first loves! That meant something! I'll have a single red rose, I said, walking into the florist. Do you want a ribbon? A card? With love or with sympathy? Both, I said. Both.

SIX

KAY: When was this?

SI: A few weeks ago. He called after the police'd arrested Arfon Jones. They'll definately be in touch now, he said. How you feeling? And he was all quiet on the other end of the phone, waiting for me to tell him something. As if I would tell that bastard anything.

KAY: I don't remember him.

SI: Yeah, you do. Your year; specky git! (*As in, he was.*)

KAY: No.

SI: You know him. I know you know him.

KAY: Glasses?

SI: Yeah.

KAY: No.

SI: Forget it, he's just a twat. He just came out with all this truth shit and I didn't want to know. Even though I always knew if I came home, it'd all come out; shit would hit! (*Pause.*) You know, I was almost legal when it happened.

KAY: What do you mean?

SI: I was seventeen. He could almost have called me the friend he thought I was. They were my friends, he said when they cross-examined him. Why did they betray me? As if he was Jesus Christ.

KAY: Oh, I'm sorry, Si...

SI: Why? It wasn't your fault; wasn't mine either. Though at the time, I thought it was, that's why I couldn't tell anyone.

KAY: You could've told me.

SI: No. Not then. Hard as hell now, but not then... not you... not anyone. That's why I left. You thought it was about us.

KAY: Felt like it was.

SI: I know and I felt shitty about that. But it wasn't, and you went on and on about how I was hurting you...

KAY: I know.

SI: And my mother gave me all this guilt shit. To be honest, I reckon my dad was glad to see the back of me, but he was still a git. You were all getting at me. I'd let you all down, you said. It was all you, you, you.... So how could I tell any of you what had happened to me?

KAY: I didn't understand.

SI: Do you think I did? Even now... it's just a... oh, fuck.

KAY: If you don't want to talk about it, Si.

SI: No, I want to. I've got to. I want to get it clear in my own mind before I tell the police. (*Pause.*) If you want to be a great actor, you've got to experience everything, that's what he used to say. Always the same line – looks like we all fell for it. But he was our teacher, and you believe teachers more than you do your dad, don't you? Especially *my* dad! So I believed him, because I wanted to be an actor so bad. Remember?

KAY: Yeah.

SI: Like Stanley Baker – Valleys' boy made good. So when

he said he'd help me with my auditions, speeches for drama school, I said great. Come up to my house then, he said. And I felt special, you know. All grown-up like. Going to a teacher's house after school, as if we were friends. They were my friends, he said – friends, my arse! But I trusted him, we all did, even though he got us to do some weird shit at times. I told you bits.

KAY: Bits.

SI: But we'd do whatever, because we all wanted to please him. Like there was one bit from this play called 'Equus'. There'd be two of us; one would play the horse, the other'd get off on the back of him. And you'd be taken for a ride by another kid in pants, naked if Arfon Jones could get you to do it. Being the horse was the weirdest, neighing like hell and a boy fumbling with his cock on your back. You don't think, do you? You just do it... to experience everything. To be. Or not to fucking be, there was no question. There were other pieces as well, but I've forgotten them. But I remember what it was that night up his house. 'Spring Awakening' by Frank Wedekind...

KAY: Who?

SI: It doesn't matter who. That's all that matters is that it was just another excuse for wanking. But, all right, I thought, trusting him, and I stripped down to my pants because I wanted to feel everything, as he said I should. And there I was, book in one hand touching myself with the other, lying on his lounge floor behind closed curtains; experiencing.

And I was a bit self-conscious, you know, because he was looking at me, staring hard, and not just like a teacher. And I'd seen those eyes before, in lots of places; a look I'd run a million miles away from normally. But I stayed that night, though it freaked the shit out of me, because it was for my own good, so he said. Then, after I'd finished the speech for the third time or so, not really getting it, he said we should pretend to be young kids 'awakening'. Get to the essence of the piece through improvisation.

I thought, shit, but he went straight for it, pretending to be a baby crawling towards me. And I lay there thinking, what the hell's going on? Because I wanted to experience everything, but inside I was thinking, fucking hell! And he crouched above me and started pawing me – my arms, my legs, my head, slowly working his way in, and then I froze. And he brushed over – you know, he kind of touched me; his hand sort of brushed over me, once, twice, and I couldn't move. And he kept making these coochy-coo sounds, like a bloody baby, gurgling.

KAY: What?

SI: I tell you. Then he began to really go for it, experiencing for all he was worth. Why the hell I stayed there I don't know. But you don't think the worst until it's happened, do you? He was my teacher... and so I lay there, and then he... he slipped his fingers under my pants and he started pulling them down... and then... (*nervous laugh*) oh shit...

KAY: If you don't want to...

SI: No, I have to... I have to. I owe you an explanation; I owe myself one. I've been bottling all this shit up for five years. If it was cancer, I'd be dead by now. No, I am fucking dead, well a part of me is, though not as dead as some.... (*Resolves to continue.*) He pulled down my pants right, bent over me, and he... he... he took me in his mouth. And I feel really fucking ashamed of this because...

38

because I felt... you know. I just couldn't help myself, I just felt... and I couldn't believe what was happening; what he was doing to me. And I kept thinking about you, because we were first loves and I was betraying you. And I was thinking of all our promises, our for ever and evers, but it was the end of every-fucking-thing; of all trust... all innocence... everything. Life swallowed up, fucking gobbled, stolen from me, from us. And I just lay there and I don't know why, I still can't explain why I just lay there, hating myself. I fucking hate him, the bastard fuck! I'm sorry, I'm really sorry, Kay.

KAY: It's OK.

SI: It's not OK... it's not fucking OK. Because the bastard is – I couldn't help it, I just couldn't – but I came... in his mouth. In his fucking mouth! I didn't want to but I did. Fuck, at seventeen you come standing against the washing machine. Every minute of the day, you're bursting, so I burst (*false cocky*) shot my bastard load, spunked his tonsils out.... And I've never... I have never let anybody do that to me since – nobody. Why can't I kiss you where it counts? Carol said.

KAY: Carol?

SI: Baker Street.

KAY: Oh...

SI: And when it was all over, he just got up and he was teacher-teacher again. Now use that emotion in future, he said, use that sucking emotion. And I wanted to fucking hit him, I wanted to hit him so sodding hard... but I didn't. I just got up and left. I actually thanked him. I actually thanked the fucker for fucking my life up! Would you believe it?

After that, I couldn't face him, couldn't face you or anyone. I felt dirty. Scrub-it-with-a-Brillo dirty! A few poxy moments and everything was ruined. My life was ruined in the blink of the one-eyed fucking snake. Everything!

And that's all he could say was, use that emotion! Well, that emotion has been using me every day ever since. That's why I had to get away from everyone I knew who knew nothing; move somewhere full of people who didn't need to know, and carry on as if nothing had happened, when I was dying inside.

KAY: Oh, Si...

SI: Oh, I was lucky. Just the once for me. I got away with my life, just about. Others... oh, I tell you, I had no idea... no idea. That's why I keep thinking, if only I'd said something at the time... before anyone else, because I reckon I was probably about the first... and if I'd said something then.... But who would they have believed? Him or me? He was God, I was a kid. Who could I tell? I mean, would you have believed me?

No answer.

Si: Honestly? Really honestly?

Kay shakes her head.

SI: I'm sorry, Kay. I'm really sorry, 'cause I feel responsible.

KAY: What for?

SI: For everything. If that hadn't have happened then I

wouldn't have left you, then you wouldn't have met Craig, and all the shit that's happened, wouldn't have happened.

KAY: I'm glad I met him. I love my little Ry, Si.

SI: I know that, what I mean is...

KAY: Sh... sh....

SI: Oh God.... First date for five years and I hit you with this shit.

KAY: Just hold me.

SI: (*Reluctantly*) I...

KAY: Please.

They embrace.

SI: It could all've been so different....

KAY: Stay tonight.

SI: It's late, my mother'll send a search party out.

KAY: Phone her.

SI: What would be the point? We can't change anything, can we; we can't go back.

KAY: I don't want to go back.

SI: I do.

KAY: You can't.

SI: Don't I know it.

They kiss passionately – instigated by KAY.

KAY: Come to bed.

SI: I'm not clean.

KAY: Are you diseased?

SI: Unwashed.

KAY: So am I.

They caress.

MAM: Look into my eyes, Si. Did that man try anything on with you, love?

SI: No.

MAM: Are you sure?

SI: Yes.

MAM: Not lying?

SI: No!

MAM: You wouldn't lie to your mother would you?

MAM and SI speak simultaneously:

SI: And in my lie, lay the truth of our family – no trust, no love, just fear. And we're not special. We're just like so many other families who spend their whole lives afraid of bursting into flames, and the fear becomes so normal, so bloody natural, you don't think you could live without it. And kids grow up smouldering, and look for other petrol marriages so that they can fire up. Fear burning through the generations, unchecked... all consuming, bush fires in New South Wales....

MAM: To be honest, Bri, I didn't want to hear the true truth. Not about Si. It would've meant that I'd betrayed him; been betrayed myself. It would've upset everything; raked up all sorts of stuff, all swept under the carpet. Everything we were and are, our whole lives dragged out in the open. Who in their right mind would want to do that, eh? Let sleeping dogs lie, as my mam used to say. Life's hard enough as it is. A little white fib never hurt no one, did it, Bri?

Moment. MAM and SI no longer speak simultaneously.

MAM: Tell me, love, and I won't ask you again, I promise. Did anything happen?

SI: No.

MAM: And he didn't blink, he didn't blink, Bri! And I was glad, because the truth would've killed me.

SEVEN

KAY and SI are post-coital.

KAY: Do you remember that Sunday, when we walked the long way to the top of Pen y Fan? Do you remember? Up that valley and there was no one around, so we lay down on the heather and we made love. And all those buzzards flying above us.

SI: Yeah. And what about that time with your tights on, just to see if it worked, and your toes curled up each time I pushed in.

KAY: Please...

SI: Back alley in Wattstown. Back of a bus to Porthcawl...

KAY: And when you climbed onto the shed and into my bedroom in my Gran's house, and you left before dawn just like James Bond.

SI: On Her Majesty's Secret Service, I was.

KAY: She heard you.

SI: Never.

KAY: Told me before she died.

SI: You're kidding.

KAY: Honest.

SI: Shit... and what about that time in the Mini...

KAY: That wasn't me.

SI: Wasn't it? Should've been.

Pause.

KAY: Did you love Lucy, Si?

SI: Did you love Craig?

KAY: I asked first.

SI: Not fair.

KAY: Did you?

SI: Don't know. I think I loved the idea of her more than her.

KAY: What?

SI: Everything was easy for her. Nice house, nice car, swimming pool, good school, best university. She'll probably marry some bloody Crispin in a Norman church. And they'll have a reception in a marquee full of kids with parents all dressed in linen. Do not pass go, go straight to heaven. Yeh, I would've liked to have had all that. Wouldn't you?

KAY: Would you!

SI: Well. at least I would've liked the choice not to have wanted it. Know what I mean?

Pause.

KAY: You've always been a snob, Si.

SI: No way. My grandfather was a card-carrying Communist.

KAY: Whose wasn't?

SI: I'm talking about choice, that's all. I mean, wouldn't you have wanted all that?

KAY:? I just wanted to dance around a handbag for ever.

SI: Well, that was your choice.

KAY: I had no choice, Si.

SI: I'm sorry.

KAY: We're always sorry.

SI: The sorry people, the could've beens.

KAY: Could you have been happier with me?

SI: Don't know what I could've been.

KAY: I know you, and I know one thing...

SI: What?

KAY: You woudn't have been any happier with me.

SI: How come?

KAY: It just would've ended with a Bacardi Breezer in Ponty instead of a Pimms in Chelsea; different drink, same difference.

SI: No, it would've been different with us, we would've been different.

KAY: Would've? So we're history already? I thought we'd only just begun again.

Pause.

SI: Will be, then. Remember a dusty garage?

KAY: You said I smelled of wee.

SI: Pee on me now.

KAY: What!

SI: I want to taste you.

KAY: Is this a pervy London thing?

SI: Pure Valleys rain. Shower me.

Over the next speech, KAY urinates into SI's mouth. Afterwards they kiss, then KAY goes down on SI. He is nervous but eventually relents. She kisses him throughout his speech.

MAM: Do you remember when we were younger, Bri? Before we had kids? You'd take me dancing down The Rink, and you'd fling me 'round the dancefloor like a rag doll and I'd be flying. Before we were married, we had fun. Do you remember fun, Bri? Long time ago now; another life. The Rink's been knocked down this year, hasn't it? Turned into a garage. Shame....

I tell you what though, when you get out, we'll have a big party up the Res, eh? We'll have a dance. It'll be like that film, 'Scent of a Woman'. We'll have a wheelchair tango. You and me on the dance floor again. You lead, I'll follow. Would you like that, love? One blink for yes? Two for no. Yes? No. Please Bri, I'm trying very hard here. It's not easy, Brian. It's not easy and you're not helping none. You've never helped. You should've shot me, not the bloody crow! Pawn this ring, buy back the gun. I'll do it myself – two birds with one bullet; mercy killing. Don't close your eyes on me, you bastard. Don't you dare. Don't you dare, Brian! I hate you....

SI: The whole truth and nothing but the truth made me think harder; remember the detail. Day of the week, hour of the night. Did anything else happen? The tears inside as I walked out the front door, got on my motorbike and screamed the valley, canyon wide.

And sometime during the interview an officer burst in, and I sort of guessed from the look on his face that something had gone down. And later, on the news, they said the police had found him hanged in his cell, and I realised then that I would never get the chance to point my finger and accuse the bastard! He was probably scared shitless for his soft arse behind bars!

And because he'd topped himself, arseholes would always be able to doubt the words of us abused, because Arfon Jones was an inspiration, they'd say, an inspi-fucking-ration, and you can't find a dead man guilty, can you? The manipulator of little boys played with cocks and minds from beyond the grave. And what about us! We needed some sort of release... some justice. But we'll always be strung up by our balls and tits as if we'd invited the abuse!

They were... my friends... your honour. Friends... my arse! We needed exorcism... not Jamie Owen on the news – more English than Edwards – smiling as he announced a bastard's suicide, as off... hand... as if... a dog... had... just... died... in... Dinas! (*He climaxes.*) Oh God... bastard God....

EIGHT

SI: Fancy a pint down the Colliers? Got something I want to talk about, my brother said after the weather. More sodding rain! My shout, he said. Put the flags out! Piss off. Family charm. I see you take after dad. Yeah, well, I'm proud of that even if you're not, he said, cutting me down. We took the short cut through the alley where the milkman's dog once bit my leg. Life's a bitch like that, innit? He said. Get it? Yeah I got it, Kev.

In the bar, I sat and he said, his said. It's been nearly a year now and the police are none the wiser, right? Right, Kev. That's all they care about are speeding fines and fucking boxing! So you keep saying, Kev. Yeah, well it's true, right. They don't give a toss about little people like us! So I reckon the only way we get justice in this world, is to fight for it! I tell you now, Si, I'm going to find out who nicked Dad's van and I'm going to get him. No mercy. It's up to you and me, bro! So what do you say? I'm not sure. Fuck's sake, mun. It's all gone shit since the van was stolen, right? One moment of fuckery has ruined everything. Dad'll never be the same again, and Mam... it's killing her, mun. Kills me to watch her. No one has the right to get away with something like that. The police don't have to sit in that hospital every day and watch her cracking up and him just lying there like a turd. There's no hope, mun; no justice! It's up to you and me to fight for it. So you keep saying, Kev. Yeah well, I'm saying it again.

Now, I don't mean this funny right, but if you love Mam and Dad and you want to make up for all the pain you've caused them – no you wait. None of that big bro shit now, just hear me out. If you really care about Mam and Dad, you'll help me nail the little bastard who did this. Porth's small, someone's bound to know something and I'm going to make it my business to find out who dumped us in it, even if it's the last thing I do. Someone's going to pay, big fucking time! So, are you in or are you in?

NINE

KAY: Is it Sunday tomorrow, Mam? All day, love. Will Si take us to Porthcawl as he promised? Will he, Mam? If I can borrow your uncle Steve's car he will. Now go to sleep, that's a good boy, Bogeyman's coming....

SI: Sunday best, Sunday dinner, Sunday school, then up to Gran's for Sunday tea – all trifle, cakes and bloody jelly, and I'd be hot as hell with sugar; all geared up with nowhere to go. Then I'd have a bath before 'Family Fortunes' and I'd be sent up the wooden hill whilst it was still light outside. And I'd lie in bed, wide awake, listening to the sound of the Evans' stinking out the street, laughing at all the clean kids, tucked up, waiting for Monday morning to come. Sundays, always smelled of dog shit bleaching in the sun; nothing ever happened....

MAM: I went to Chapel this morning, love. Then back home to cook dinner for the boys so I could get here by three. Just another Sunday really...

SI: Not just another Sunday; a year to the day the van was stolen; a shitty anniversary. When I woke up this morning, I knew something smelled wrong; the day smelled almost fresh....

MAM: Simon's gone to Porthcawl with Kay and her kid. Do you remember when we went to Porthcawl before we were married, Bri? We stayed in Aunty Vera's caravan. Remember? Forgotten all ready have you, love? That's convenient! We were having such a lovely time of it until Wednesday, when you started an argument about the chips. One of those arguments about nothing you always loved so much. And I said if you're going to be so pathetic I'm going to catch the bus home. And you said, go on then, if you want to spoil the holiday. As if you hadn't spoiled it enough already! So I caught the bus home. And that night I waited for you, thinking you'd come home and apologise, but you didn't. And the next day I waited, and the next. I waited all week! But you stayed in the caravan on your own, if you please! Had to get my money's worth, you said. Brian, we never paid for that holiday, it was for free! And you've never apologised to me for that.. never. I've hated Porthcawl ever since – can't stand it. I only used to go there for the boys.

KAY: Porthcawl was perfect. Si was great with Ry. Like a dad should be. I know I shouldn't have thought that, but I did, and you do, don't you. He built a castle, big enough for Ry to sit in. And as the tide began to come in, Ry kept plugging the gaps, but it was no use, it all melted away until, in the end, he was sitting in a hole where his castle had been, tears of sand running down his cheeks, poor little dab. We had to drag him away crying, all the way to the fair...

SI: Past the Grand National where a perv gave me the eye when I was twelve. Lick of rock, little boy...

KAY: And Ryan ate all sorts of junk and broke the bank on the bouncy castle. And then he cried again because he didn't want to leave. He wanted the day to go on and on for a month of Sundays. We all did.

SI: Don't cry now...

KAY: There'll be other days, Si said. Now, who wants an ice cream? Me me me! And we were all laughing and licking Fulgonis as we walked along the prom, Ryan walking between us, playing happy families. And I bought us a bag of scrimps for the way home. It was a perfect day. Lou Reed could've sung about it.

SI: And I was singing 'Green grow the rushes ho' as we passed the whispering angel in Blackmill on the way home. Sh! Ryan love, sh! But I want to pee, he said. Can't you wait until we get home? I'm desperate. Thin voice, thin streak of piss against the back wheel of the car, one hand on the bodywork, all legal like.

KAY: And remember to shake it before you put it back in, like the big boys do.

SI: Yeah, of course I do, Ry. I'm a big boy now. Finished? Now jump back into the car, kid. And we were all ready to pick up 'Ten for the Ten Commandments' when I turned the key in the ignition.

KAY: And as he turned the key, the sun hid.

SI: Nothing happened. I turned it again, still nothing. Twat!

KAY: Yes, Ryan. Tract.

SI: Yeah, your uncle's a tract, a big tract, kid!

KAY: He said he'd been having a bit of trouble with the alternator.

SI: When did he tell you this?

KAY: This morning, when I took the keys.

SI: Is he AA? RAC?

KAY: Steve! (*As in, what do you think?*)

SI: Shit.

KAY: He was going to fix it tomorrow.

SI: Great! Stuck in Blackmill overnight, whispering with the dead. On the other hand, an altenator's an alternator, no big deal, I thought. I just needed something heavy to hit it with. So I got out of the car, opened the bonnet, then went round to the boot to see if he had any tools, and thank God, there was this monkey wrench there. A brand new monkey wrench in a busted up car, brilliant. So there I was, tapping the alternator, Kay was turning over the engine and in the end we got it going. And I slammed down the bonnet, chucked the wrench in the boot, and I was about to close it, when I noticed something on the handle of the wrench. I didn't put two and two together at first. Well, you don't, do you? And then I twigged. I picked the wrench back up and held it as if it was a precious relic, a bastard miracle or something. Because there on the handle was the name 'Brian Voel and Son' – my father and Kevin. And I picked up a few more tools from the boot and they were all marked the same. My father's tools! Everything he'd worked for all his life and all the pain of the past twelve months, thrown and forgotten in my lover's brother's dirty, oily, shitty boot. How's your dad? He asked one night in the Colliers, like one of those blokes on TV who makes an appeal for an abducted kid, when only he knows where the corpse is hid. How's your fucking dad, my arse! I put the tools carefully back in the boot and got in the car. Anything the matter? Kay asked. No. 'Ten for the Ten Cumamments', Si? I'm sung out, kid.

MAM: It's getting late. Time goes, doesn't it; falls to bits, disappears. Remember that trick Ken did once in John and Maria's? Remember? You were jealous as hell.... Ken took that paper you find on one of those almondy biscuits, made a tube of it and lit it. And as it burnt down I thought, hell! He'll burn a hole in the lovely white table cloth! But, at the last moment, it rose up into the air like magic. A miracle it was. And I caught it in my hand as it floated down, and I could hardly feel the ash – so delicate, it was – then you blew, and it fell to bits. Funny.... It's Ken's funeral tomorrow morning. You and him were so close. Only fifty-six, makes you think, doesn't it.... Such a waste.

TEN

SI: Is he sleeping?

KAY: Totally whacked out. Today meant a lot to him, Si.

SI: I enjoyed it.

KAY: Did you?

SI: It was great.

KAY: You had a face like a slapped arse on the way home.

54

SI: Did I?

KAY: You went all funny on us.

SI: I didn't.

KAY: Ryan noticed.

SI: There was nothing to notice.

KAY: Why is Si crack, mam, he said?

SI: I wasn't.

KAY: Look, if it's about the car...

SI: Forget it.

KAY: I'm sorry.

SI: It wasn't the car.

KAY: Why did you go funny, then?

SI: No reason.

KAY: Why spoil a perfect day then?

SI: It's this talent I've got, runs in the family.

KAY: Don't be funny, Si. Just tell me. What was it?

SI: Nothing.

KAY: Why is it always nothing with you, Si?

SI: I don't want to talk about it.

KAY: So there is something then...

SI: Leave it, please.

KAY: Si, you always do this.

SI: Do what?

KAY: I'm a big girl now, Si. I don't do shit any more. Just tell me.

SI: It's no big deal.

KAY: Tell me then.

SI: I...

KAY: You what?

SI: I... (*Exhales.*)

KAY: Spit it out, will you.

SI: Don't stress me, OK?

KAY: Just tell me.

SI: All right! (*He finds it hard.*) Why?

KAY: Why what?

SI: No, where...

KAY: Where what?

SI: Where did your brother get his tools from?

KAY: Tools?

SI: The ones in the boot of his car.

KAY: I don't know. Bought them, I expect.

SI: Where?

KAY: Tool shop.

SI: You sure?

KAY: Does it matter?

SI: Yeah.

KAY: Tool envy?

SI: It's not funny.

KAY: All right.

SI: I'm serious, Kay.

KAY: All right, if it's that important I'll ring him now and find out.

KAY goes towards the phone. SI stops her.

SI: No, don't.

KAY: Do you want to know, or don't you?

SI: I do.

KAY: Right.

SI: But...

KAY: But what?

SI: Look, forget about it. I shouldn't have said anything.

KAY: Oh, for God's sake.

SI: I'm probably jumping the gun anyway.

KAY: About what?

No response.

KAY: About what!

SI: About your brother's tools.

KAY: What about them?

SI: I said forget about them.

KAY: Si. You're like a bloody cracked record. Stop pissing about and tell me. What is it?

Pause.

SI: All right.... I think they were my dad's tools.

KAY: Your dad's! Are you sure?

SI: I know they were his. I could tell.

KAY: How?

SI: His name was on them.

KAY: His name?

SI: Brian Voel and Son. Big letters on the handles.

KAY: You're joking?

SI: I wish.

KAY: Oh my God...

SI: (*With hesitation*) Do you know anything about this?

KAY: Oh, come on...

SI: Not that I don't trust you or anything.

KAY: No, I don't.

SI: No?

KAY: Don't you believe me?

SI: Yeah, of course, but...

KAY: But what?

SI: You might know how he got hold of them, that's all.

KAY: Don't you dare! Look, Si, I'll talk to him, right.

SI: I'll do it.

KAY: No, let me talk to him.

SI: I said I'll do it.

KAY: Let me talk to him first, Si. I'll deal with this my way. OK? And, I promise, if I think for a moment he stole the van, I'll call the police myself.

SI: No way. He's not getting away with it. Because that's what will happen if the police get hold of him. They won't do him. Lack of evidence, they'll say. Then I'll never be able to get at him, because he'll call it harassment if I do. So we'll do it my way. He's your brother, but it's my father dying in that bastard hospital.

KAY: I know it is.

SI: Your brother's always been a twat anyway!

KAY: Oh, come on!

SI: Admit it.

KAY: Look, keep your voice down, will you, Si. Ryan's sleeping.

SI: I'm not shouting.

KAY: You are.

SI: I'm not.

KAY: You are.

SI: Look, I don't want to argue with you, right. I'll be back later.

KAY: Si, listen...

SI: He's probably up the Con Club, isn't he?

KAY: I don't know where he is.

SI: Sunday night, must be.

KAY: Si, please...

SI: No.

KAY: If you love me...

SI: What's that got to do with it.

KAY: If you love me...

SI: I was abused. I don't know what love is.

KAY: Don't talk shit. If you love me, Si, don't go. Please.

KAY embraces SI. SI pulls away.

SI: Do I make you come?

KAY: What?

SI: Do I make you come when we make love?

61

KAY: Yes.

SI: Don't lie.

KAY: Don't be a shit.

SI: Do I?

RYAN: (*Calling for KAY from upstairs*) Ma-am...

KAY: See, you've woken him. Mam'll come and tuck you in now, love.

SI: Well?

KAY: You do.

SI: Sure?

KAY: Don't be a bastard.

SI: Don't shit me.

KAY: Please, Si...

RYAN: Mam!

KAY: Be there now, love. Si...

KAY goes to grab SI. SI pulls away.

SI: Back later.

KAY: I'm warning you, Si. Don't do it...

SI: Do what?

RYAN: Mam!

KAY: Mam's coming now, love. Si?

RYAN: Mam!

KAY: Put a sock in it, will you Ry!

SI: Be back later.

KAY: I mean it, Si.

SI: Whatever.

KAY: Don't ruin everything, Si. He's not worth it.

RYAN: Ma-am!

SI leaves.

KAY: Shit! Stupid little shit!

RYAN: Who's a shit, mam?

KAY: No one, Ry.

RYAN: Dad's outside the window again, Mam!

KAY: Dad's dead, love.

KAY reaches for her mobile phone as MAM closes the curtain and puts on lipstick.

MAM: Let me shut the door tight, pull the blinds, close the curtains so as the nurses can't see us. Time for one last dance. Eh, love?

KAY: Answer the phone... answer the bloody phone. For God's sake, pick it up! Will you pick up the bastard phone, you twat!

ELEVEN

SI: I ran past the zebra where my father went down, past Devonalds and the old police station, down to Porth Square. Perhaps I should've turned left up the hill to the Colliers where my brother was, but I wanted to keep him out of it for his own sake, for my mother's sake. So I turned right towards Dinas and the Con Club.

I'd guessed right, because there he was, lining up a shot on the table furthest from the door. Six or seven friends hunched under the weight of the smoke and the overhead light.

I sat in the shadows, watching him. I reckon he'd already sussed the spanner in the boot because he looked at me, miscued and lost his game. Then he reached for his mobile phone and I saw him dial one and listen. I saw his face change from spring to winter, no sun between. He looked towards me and I knew then that Kay'd warned him. Slowly, he put his phone back into his pocket. Deliberate like. I saw him mouth the word 'bog' to his friend and he was gone. I let a few seconds pass, then went in after him.

But when I got there, he'd gone! He'd slipped out through the window like a turd out of an hole, so I slipped out after him. Which way did he go? I shouted at a kid who was poking a shitty stick at nothing. But I didn't need directions, I could hear his footsteps echo around the Sunday valley; pounding the dead air.

I followed him across the square, down Station St and across the railway bridge to the other side of the tracks. Then we threaded through the lanes at the back of North Rd and came out just by the Llwyncelyn. And as he crossed the road on the humpbacked bridge, a car nearly ran him over. He fell, picked himself up and limped into the garage forecourt where The Rink had once stood.

During the next speech, DAD rises from his bed and begins to dance with MAM. By the end, she has mounted him and they make love.

MAM: Come on, Bri. Dance with me, love, like you used to. Take me down The Rink when we first met. One last ride whilst the nurses aren't looking. Start your engine. 750cc Bonneville, my Triumph! Take me for a spin, up the tip and back again! For better or for worse; four stroke engine; crafted for an easy ride.

I'm clutching on, clutch out, love. Throttle me, throttle back. Let's cruise through Porth, with the warm wind in my hair. And if the nurse catches us, who cares, we'll ride off into the sunset together. Check mirror, indicate, let's scream off up Little America, past Pentregwynt, up up and away, hanging on by my wits' ends. And we'll arrive just in time, love, just as the smooch is about to begin. Hold me tight, love. Hold me close; close as close can be, Bri. Please, Bri, please... dance me Bri, spin me to heaven....

The light fades slowly on the lovers.

TWELVE

SI: The last dance, a slow number, circling 'round an empty Tesco carrier; handbag dancing Valleys style. Then quicker, as words began to beat the rhythm; bass to the heart.

Did you steal my Dad's van? Did you? Where did you get his tools from then? Tell me. Found them? Found them where? They found you. Oh yeah, and I'm supposed to believe that, am I? Am I? You're a walking lie, you shit. What! Now that's polite, isn't it! Just tell me where you got the tools from? Jewson! Juice my fucking arse! Where did you get the tools from, you git? What do you mean they were in the car when you bought it? You've had the car two years, the van was only stolen a year ago tonight. Two and two don't make three. Don't piss on me or I'll piss on you from a height. Now, where did you get them from? Beats you, eh? Beats the shit out of me!

And I looked at him, and guilt marked him like a spider tattoo. Look at me. I said look at me! You did it, didn't you? I know it was you. It's written on your face, a face to fucking fart in if ever there was one! It was you, wasn't it? What? You guilty fuck! You hurt my family, I'll hurt you – Muerta in the fucking Valley!

He turned and I lunged after him, grabbed him by the neck, and started squeezing. But you don't get a good grip from behind, you need thumbs to the throat. So he hit me with a rabbit to my ribs and I fell away, not expecting the hit. I thought he'd throw up his arms and scream fair cop! But he wouldn't go down without a fight. So we squared up and I felt his breath condense on my face. Why did you do it? I shouted. Why did you do it?

His chest bouncing on my fists. Why, you fuck arse? Why did you do it? For the crack! He shouted back. For a laugh, he laughed, because I felt like it! (*Thrown.*) You what? Because you felt like it! What the shit does that mean? You ruined my bastard family because, one night, you passed the house and thought, I just feel like it! What the hell do you mean you felt like it? What made you feel like it? Why did you do it? Why the fuck? You fucking dick wipe! And I grabbed him by the lapels and shook the truth screaming out of him. Because you farted in my face! He said. (*He reels as he comprehends.*) What! The music stopped. A dog barked. Because you farted in my face. So what! And you shagged my sister in the next room when you thought I wasn't listening. That's why I felt like it.

Shit! I should've decked him, forehead to the nose and sent him down, because he floored me; floored my family. I should've hammered my fist into him, boot to the body, made him piss sorries from his mouth; all the sorries from all the suckers and fuckers who ever hurt me; all red apologies and smashed teeth. I should've strung sense out on a wire of expletives and strangled him with it. That's what my Dad would've done, I owed him the flattery of imitation at least. I owed him something, didn't I?

I could've turned the other cheek. Moved to the moral high ground. I could've sneered from an 'ight, but shit, my grandfather was a card-carrying Communist, how could I do that!

I should've done something, but I didn't. I just looked at him as the crows circled above. And in that moment of hesitation, he knew he had me beat. I shagged his sister, so he sucked the cock of my family and I was too much of a... what was I? What am I? My father's prodigal, Arfon Jones' prodigy, a tragedy dying to happen? Sins fucking revisited! Whatever.... I stood rooted in what I could've been, in what I never will be, and I let him dance all over me scot-free into the night. I let him dance into the night.... I should've... I know I should've... but I didn't. I fucking didn't. I'm a walking could've-bastard-been.... Look at my fucking shoes – cheap as chips... cheap as fucking chips.

THIRTEEN

(*Mam is straightening her dress*)

MAM: It's not your fault, Bri. You're just under the weather, love. It's probably me. Blame me for it – you've blamed me for everything else down the years. Frigid cow, it's your bastard fault. Always my fault. Eh, Bri? What do you say? Nothing? Silence is golden, as my mam used to say. Damn! I've got a ladder in my tights....

We should've divorced a long time ago, but you don't, do you? You put up with it, even though every day hammers you a little bit more; Hammer House of Horror our house was. Scream and an' half! We should've parted a long time ago whilst the going was still half good, it would've been better for both of us.

But it's too late now, isn't it? It wouldn't be right to divorce a dying man, would it? Shame on me, there'd be talking. For better or for worse, we said. Are we sure we said it? Is there a video? Any proof? Mm?

I like this new silence. I can speak in it. And you can't cut me off, you have to listen, must be hell for you. But fair's fair, it's been hell for me for years. You've no idea how much you've hurt me, Bri, no idea at all.

And not that I want to hurt you back, I just want to get a few things off my chest, that's all. Because there shouldn't be any secrets between husband and wife, should there, Bri? No?

Truth is, you've never made me happy, Bri, not in that way. I'm sorry to have to tell you now. But the thing is, it's not my fault. And I know it's not my fault. And do you know why? Because I was happy once. Only a little moment it was, a long time ago, but it's kept me going all these years.

Remember the time you went to hospital; ingrowing hair up your backside. You were so ashamed, when you

68

came home you took me from behind, cold and dry just to prove you were still a man. And that was the night you thought Simon was conceived. But, ignorance is bliss. Guess who said that? Eh, Bri? Wrong.

Ken's always been a good friend of yours, hasn't he? Go up and check on Jean for me whilst I'm in hospital, will you, Ken? See if she wants anything, will you, Ken? Do anything for you. You were so close. To be honest, before we were married, I thought you were both gay! Oh, wash my mouth.

Anyway, he came round one evening, as you'd asked him to. That afternoon, you'd shot me down for something or other, as usual, and I was crying when he called. And Ken dried my tears and we played our own game of doctors and nurses. And as you lay on your stomach in hospital with your arse stuck in the air, I lay back in our bed and Ken made me happy. And you know what? I didn't feel guilty one bit, I was happy as a pig in shit, honest! Because I realised then, that it wasn't me that was to blame for every-bloody-thing in this world, not that I was blame free, just that I wasn't Mrs Bloody Guilty.

The ward bell rings.

MAM: There, see, time's gone quick today, hasn't it? Time flies when you're having fun, eh? You see, Brian Voel – master plumber – whatever you've said over the years, there's never been anything wrong with my pipes. It's just that you're a bad workman, always blaming your tools. Just the once, but you can't forget something like that, can you? It carries you through all the bad times, the long years I've had to jump to his master's voice. To be honest, I wouldn't have told you Bri, but nothing focuses the mind like a death does it? Truth is, Brian, Si's not your son, he's not your boy... he's Ken's. And, however dead you've made me feel, at least I know, I lived for a moment. And in that precious moment, Si was made. His dad's funeral's in the morning, so I'd better go. I'll be late for visiting tomorrow. I'll say a prayer for you both....

MAM kisses DAD.

SI: My mother'd gone by the time I arrived at the hospital. The wards were closed. I begged the sister to let me in, said I was leaving for the city in the morning; wanted to say goodbye to him in case anything happened.

Dad? It's me. I bloody know it's you, his eyes cut me down into the chair beside him. The lights were low, his heart monitor was bleeping. Dad? Are you listening? He closed his eyes. I wanted to tell him things, explain away my life, or bloody excuse for one, as he would say. I wished I could tell him how I avenged his death, like some Sicilian made man, and made good the family name. I wanted him to be proud of me, if only for a moment. One of those brief moments that change a life, but he was changing nothing. You'd have thought a father would've been proud of his son if only because he was flesh and blood. My father was stone, there was no point squeezing him.

So the two of us sat there in silence for some minutes; painfully aware of the lack that lay between us; a canyon of nothing between father and son which grew wider and wider by the minute. Soon, we wouldn't be able to see each other, just the memory of where the edges used to be.

And the silence was killing. How many deaths had I endured with him? How many more would I have to endure if I stayed? I'll be off to Balham in the morning, I said. Time for me to wake up and smell the coffee, eh! So, before leaving, I just wanted to say... and he opened his eyes, looked into mine for the longest time, then blinked. And I saw one small tear leave the sanctuary of his eye and fall down his cheek. Was it compassion? Was it love? Contempt? Was it hate? Whatever it was, it was too late, way way too late? Goodbye, Dad. Go gentle. Good night.

KAY has finished the wreath. SI flips the switch on the life support. Silence. Darkness.

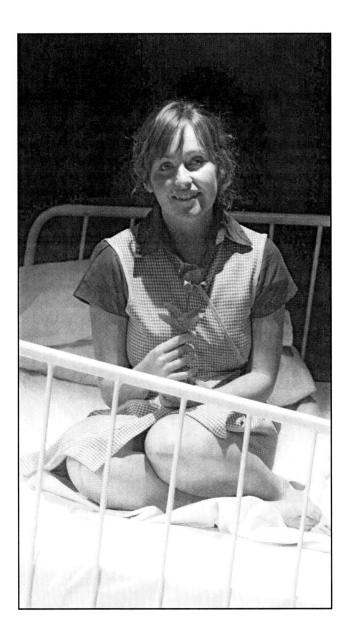

Director

Stephen Fisher was born in London, in 1965. He began directing at University of Wales, Swansea, where he achieved a BA honours degree in Drama & English. On graduating he co-founded a physical theatre company and created a number of works that toured the UK and Europe. He subsequently wrote and performed several solo theatre pieces, whilst also working as an actor and in production for radio, film and television.

From 2000-04 he was Associate Director at the Sherman Theatre, Cardiff, during which time his original production of *Saturday Night Forever* by Roger Williams played in New York as part of the 'UK with NY' festival.

He has worked with many Welsh theatre companies, including the National Theatre (theatr Genedlaethol Cymru), Fiction Factory, Theatre Clwyd, Script Cymru, Theatr na n'Og and Torch Theatre. He regularly teaches and directs at universities including Trinity College Carmarthen, Newport Film School and the Royal Welsh College of Music & Drama.

Stephen set up F.A.B. Theatre with the intention of creating high quality productions of the best Welsh theatre.

Theatre Companies

F.A.B. Theatre is a new company. Its founding members are Steve Fisher, Artistic Director, and Emma Goad, Producer. Between them they have over thirty years experience of professional theatre making. Whilst based in Cardiff, their work has been seen in America, Australia, across Europe and throughout the UK.

The Torch is a celebrated producing theatre company that boasts an impressive repertoire including *One Flew Over The Cuckoo's Nest*, *Neville's Island*, *Abigail's Party*, *The Little Shop of Horrors*, *Of Mice and Men* and *Educating Rita*. The Torch Theatre in Milford Haven celebrated its 30th anniversary in 2007 with an ambitious refurbishment which has transformed it into one of the most comfortable venues in the British Isles.

Printed in the United Kingdom
by Lightning Source UK Ltd.
130011UK00001B/19-141/P